# Dino Love

**Michelle Worthington**

**Veronica Montoya**

LOVE is . . .

# Dino ♥ Love

To Tom, who will never stop
loving dinosaurs ~ M W

Thanks to New Frontier for giving me the opportunity
to illustrate this wonderful story about the diversity
of love, families and the value of friendship ~ V M

CATCH a STAR

First published in the UK in 2020 by Catch a Star,
an imprint of New Frontier Publishing Europe Ltd
Uncommon, 126 New King's Rd, London SW6 4LZ
www.newfrontierpublishing.co.uk

Text © Michelle Worthington 2020 • Illustrations © Veronica Montoya 2020

ISBN: 978-1-912858-97-2

A CIP record for this book is available from the British Library

Designed by Verity Clark
Printed in China

13 5 7 9 10 8 6 4 2

. . . goodbye hugs.

. . . saying 'I'll miss you.'

... feeling grown up.

Love is . . .

. . . taking deep breaths.

...doing your best.

...never giving up.

Love is . . .

...big.

. . . small.

...different shapes

and colours.

Love is how you feel
on the inside.

LOVE is all.